PENGUIN BOOKS

THE TRIPLE ECHO

Born in 1905, H. E. Bates was educated at Kettering Grammar School and worked as a journalist before publishing his first book, *The Two Sisters,* when he was twenty. In the next fifteen years he won a distinguished reputation for his stories about English country life. In 1941, as 'Flying Officer X', he wrote his two famous books of short stories – *The Greatest People in the World* and *How Sleep the Brave* – which were followed in 1944 by *Fair Stood the Wind for France.* These, and his subsequent novels of Burma, *The Purple Plain* and *The Jacaranda Tree,* and of India, *The Scarlet Sword,* stemmed directly or indirectly from his war experience in the East, won him a new reputation and, apart from their success in Britain and America, have been translated into sixteen foreign languages. His writing took a new direction with the appearance in 1958 of *The Darling Buds of May*, the first of the popular Larkin family novels, which was followed by *A Breath of French Air, When the Green Woods Laugh*, and *Oh! To be in England* (1963). *A Lover's Flowers* (1971) is his most recent book.

H. E. BATES

THE TRIPLE ECHO

Drawings by Ron Clarke

PENGUIN BOOKS

Penguin Books Ltd, Harmondsworth, Middlesex, England
Penguin Books Australia Ltd, Ringwood, Victoria, Australia

—

First published by Michael Joseph 1970
Published in Penguin Books 1972

—

Made and printed in Great Britain by
C. Nicholls & Company Ltd
Set in Monotype Baskerville

'My husband's a prisoner with the Japs. I'll probably never see him again. That's all I know.'

The farm was one of those small half-lost farms that are cut off from main roads in summer by dense barriers of beech and chestnut and repeatedly in winter by mud and fog and snow. The red-brick two-storied house and its one barn had once been thatched. Now both had a roof of corrugated iron that shone harsh grey in the summer sun and lay on them in winter like a rusting, crumbling crown.

The war was already nearly three years old when Alice Charlesworth started the hard slog of running the place herself. Even before her husband was a prisoner with the Japs all she had for company was a cow, a couple of dozen hens and a terrier that hunted the rats that infested the hen-run. The blow of losing her husband to the Japs was followed by the blow of losing the terrier when it severed a leg in a gin-trap she had set for hares. She promptly shot the dog with a double-barrelled shot-gun and after that she was quite alone except for the hens, the cow and the rats that she shot too as they came out to prowl in the hour before darkness.

She looked, if anything, rather older than her twenty-seven years. She had thick cottony black hair. She always wore dull brown denim trousers and a thick dark green sweater. Her black gum-boots were always caked with mud. The oak-brown skin of her face and arms was rough. Her eyes too were brown. Normally they were keen and warm, but sometimes as she stared down the white chalk hillside at the vast expanse of valley below they also had something of the lost glassiness seen in the eyes of birds imprisoned in cases, with only dead grass and ferns for company.

Most evenings she got into the habit, like the rats, of prowling about the place. She always carried the shot-gun. The first fears of German invasion were over by that time but, she told herself, you never knew. If there were no unexpected parachutists to shoot at there was always the danger of two-legged foxes after the hens. Food was getting scarce. Nowadays everybody was nicking things.

She had also grown intensely, almost fiercely jealous about her few acres of land. Isolation had made her suspicious of every shaking leaf or bough. At the far end of the path was a post-box nailed to a tree-trunk. She walked down to it perhaps once a week, looking vainly for letters that never came. She had long since cancelled her newspapers. The only news she got was from a small portable radio. She hardly ever had time for that either but now and then some comic or other made her laugh.

One evening in May she walked farther down the hillside than usual. It was already daylight at that time until after ten o'clock. The air after a long warm day had exceptional softness. Big white trees of hawthorn lay dotted about the valley like soft woollen puff-balls and from over the crest of the hillside, from the depths of the beech-woods, flowed a continual exquisite breath of great lakes of bluebells in flower. The war seemed a million miles away.

When she at last got back to the farm-yard, ready to shut up the hens for the night, she was suddenly aware of the figure of a man disappearing towards the woods, behind a stack of hay.

She was quick to raise the shot-gun and started running. She caught another glimpse of the man climbing a stile. Another two-legged fox, she told herself, and shouted:

'Here, you there! What's the big idea, traipsing all over other people's property?'

He stopped and turned. She was still running as he

turned but suddenly she stopped too. Gun still raised, she found herself face to face with a thin, boyish young soldier.

'What the blazes you think you're up to? Nicking something I shouldn't wonder.'

He started to mutter something about losing his way. His intensely pale blue eyes seemed scared. He was carrying his forage cap tucked in a shoulder strap. His fair light hair shone almost white.

'What you doing up here, on other folk's land? Don't they give you nothing to do in the army nowadays?'

'Walking. That's all. Just walking.'

'Funny you should walk into my place.'

'Just got lost. A bit lost –'

'Well, you can get lost again. I don't want nobody trespassing and traipsing about up here.'

'I thought there might be a way, foot-path or something, down the hill –'

'That's the only path there is. Through the wood. That way.'

She lifted the gun again, pointing it straight at him. This time he seemed more offended than scared.

'Don't you know you should never point a gun at anybody?'

'Sorry,' she said and surprised herself in saying it. 'Sorry.'

She lowered the gun. There was a good ten seconds of silence between them. Once or twice he ran his fingers through his hair. As it moved it seemed whiter than ever, almost luminous against the darkening background of tree shadow.

'You see, I –'

She found herself starting a confused explanation. Well, she was all alone up here. You never knew about people. She was always afraid there might be somebody –

'You're not afraid of me, are you?'

'I didn't say that. I didn't mean that.'

'No need to be afraid of me. I'm nobody. My name's Barton.'

All the time the light blue, boyish eyes seemed to indicate more and more that it was he, not she, who was afraid.

'I had things nicked before now. Hens. I know what soldiers are. Scrounging. On the scrounge all the time. I know. My husband's a soldier.'

'Nightingale,' he suddenly said. 'Nightingale.'

He lifted his head, listening. She could hear the nightingale too, somewhere far up, hidden in beech branches. For fully half a minute they listened to it together until at last he said:

'Marvellous, that. Marvellous.'

She said nothing.

'Haven't heard one for a long time,' he said. 'Used to have them where I come from but they've all gone now.'

'Where's that, you come from?'

'Hampshire. Like this. Not far from the sea.'

Up in the beech trees the nightingale held to one long pure sustained high note. The soldier drew in his breath and held it too.

'Nothing like it,' he said. 'They say some birds can imitate it but –'

'They sing so much I hardly seem to notice it.'

'They sing all day sometimes. Do they up here?'

'Like I said, I hardly seem to notice it.'

Now there was another long pause between them and again they listened to the nightingale. This time she broke the silence by saying:

'Sorry about the gun. I ought to have known better than that.'

Whether this embarrassed him or not she never knew. He simply said:

'We got a place like this down in Hampshire.' He looked about him for a second or two. 'Bit bigger, though. My Dad and me used to run it together. He's on his own now. Hard graft for him, all on his own.'

'I should know.'

Sharply his brilliant blue eyes turned to the direction of the high beech tops and the nightingale.

'I could listen all night to that. I could just stop and listen all night.'

To her own great surprise she actually found herself laughing.

'I can see you turning up at the guard-room,' she

said, 'with a nightingale for an excuse. What would they say to that?'

'Put me on a charge,' he said and laughed too. 'Worth it though.'

There was now yet another silence and it was she who broke it again.

'I was just going to have my supper.' She again felt conscience-stricken by her stupidity about the gun. She wanted, somehow, to make up for it. 'You could come in for a few minutes if you'd like. I'm sorry I spoke like that.'

'I don't want to take up your time –'

'Are you hungry? I've always got plenty of eggs.'

He followed her slowly, almost with shyness, into the kitchen. The table had an old green oil-cloth on it and a cup-and-saucer and plate and tea-pot left over from tea-time. She hastily cleared it and wiped the oil-cloth with a duster.

'Sit down,' she said. 'I'll put the kettle on. I generally have an egg some way or other. I'm out of bacon though. I eat the ration week-ends. Would you like poached? You can eat two, can't you?'

'Two on a raft,' he said, 'isn't that what they call it?'

'Oh! I never heard of that,' she said and laughed again. 'Sit you down. I'll lay the table.'

He sat down. By now it was growing dark. 'There's no electricity up here,' she said. 'I'll get the lamp.'

In the lamplight, as she set the lamp in the middle of

the supper-table, his eyes seemed more blue, more brilliant than ever. As often as not he kept them downcast. It was when he suddenly lifted them that they were both unbearably penetrative and at the same time shy.

While she busied herself with kettle, tea-pot, cups and eggs he barely spoke at all. But now and then he sucked at his lips and bit at them gently, as if trying to summon up courage to say something, and at last he said:

'You say your husband's a soldier?'

'Prisoner with the Japs. I'll probably never see him again. That's all I know.'

An egg cracked on the side of a cup. He seemed to catch the desolation in her voice and stared at the lamp in silence. It might have been that he wished he had never spoken. In fact he had no other word to say until she put a cup of tea and two poached eggs on a big thick square of toast in front of him.

'Thanks,' he said. 'Thanks. I don't know why you should do all this for me.'

There was nothing, she found, that she could say to that. He had no more to say either. They ate together, she rather slowly, he very quickly, swilling eggs and toast down with big gulps of tea and finally mopping up his plate with bread.

'You needed that,' she said. 'You were hungry.'

'I never thought I was but –'

'How about a repeat?'

'I –'

'Oh! eggs are things I've always got plenty of.'

She immediately left her own food and went over to the stove and started to cook eggs and make toast all over again. He watched her all the time with shy, furtive eyes, painfully blue in the lamplight.

'I see you got a tractor.'

'Fat use though. Packed up on me yesterday.'

'What's wrong with it?'

'Search me. I'm stuck with it, that's all I know. I phoned the garage up from the call-box but if I know anything about it they'll be here next Doomsday.'

Presently he was eating the second plate of eggs and toast. She poured more tea for him. Then she sat holding her own cup in her two hands, elbows on the table, not very hungry.

'I expect I could fix it.'

'Worst of machines. When they pack up they're dead. I sometimes wish I had a horse.'

'Nothing much, I expect. I'll have a look at it if you like.'

'You would? Too dark though, now.'

Well, he could come tomorrow night, he said. No trouble about that. Except when he was on guard he had the evenings off. That was why he was walking. He liked walking. Nothing else to do.

'Don't you keep very busy then?'

Farce, most of it, he said. Pointless. Parades, bull, schemes, talk about a Second Front, lot of waffle. He'd

be better off on the land. Growing something. That's where he belonged.

'You're right there. I wish –' She found herself about to say something about her husband and then abruptly decided against it and stopped: 'Well, it's all pointless.'

He was quiet again. She watched him eat. By now her own tea was getting cold and she got up to fill her cup again. Then she saw that his own cup was empty and she filled that too.

'Nice to get a good drop of tea,' he said. 'God, that army muck.'

She never once asked herself how long they sat there at the table, talking, draining the tea-pot and now and then looking furtively at each other across the lamp-light. It was only when he at last suddenly got up and said, 'Time I was going. They'll have my ears off,' that she realised how great the ache for company had been.

'Well, I'll come up tomorrow if that's all right. Will you be here tomorrow?'

'That's a laugh. Am I ever anywhere else?'

'About half seven I expect it'll be.'

She followed him into the yard outside. The far western horizon, still not completely dark, was cut across by the merest tongue of purple-orange. There were already stars.

'Thanks about the tractor,' she said. 'I'll be needing it any time now. I got a bit of early clover wants cutting.'

'Listen,' he said. 'Listen to that.'

Once again, together, they listened to the nightingale. Sometimes there were soundless, breathless pauses in the song.

After that, except when he was on guard duty or some occasional night scheme, he came to see her every evening for the next three weeks or so. In this time he repaired the tractor, sharpened the knives of the hay cutter, cut the clover, turned it and finally carried it and stacked it in the yard.

Every evening, after work, they sat in the kitchen and had supper together. They might have been husband and wife. There were always eggs and tea and toast but sometimes he scrounged a tin of bully-beef and she cooked potatoes. Once or twice, on her weekly visit to the stores at the foot of the hill, she managed to get a bottle or two of beer, a half pound of sausages, some extra cheese or even a piece of fish. Once she said:

'I had a go at a hare yesterday but I missed it by a mile.'

'You got plenty of pigeons up here. Ought to have a go at them.'

'Opportunity's a fine thing. When do you think I ever get time for pigeons?'

'All right. I'll have a go.'

But after less than a hour wandering up and down the hillside he came back, empty-handed. The gun was no good, he explained to her. All cock-eyed. You couldn't hit a church-steeple with a gun like that.

'What's wrong with it? I get the rats all right.'

'Only because you're breathing down their necks. Anyway, I'll have a good look at it when I get back.'

'Get back?'

'Off the day after tomorrow.'

She felt her heart give a dry, sudden leap. Her mouth hung open.

'Off where? You mean you're moving? Posted or something?'

'No, no,' he said and laughed. 'Leave. A whole ruddy week. Back home. Back to the farm.'

She felt her heart leap again. She pressed her lips hard together and they were dry.

'God, it'll be like ruddy heaven,' he said.

She was quiet.

'God, how I loathe it. The army, I mean. God, how I hate it. It's been like heaven up here.'

'Means I won't see you again for a bit.'

'Oh! tomorrow. I'll be up tomorrow. Then I'll be away. Crack of dawn.'

She felt the dry sudden leap in her heart again and once more she had nothing to say.

The next day, at the butcher's, she traded in two weeks' meat coupons for a piece of beef. There were new broad beans in the store and the first new potatoes. At the pub she did another trade with three dozen eggs for six bottles of beer.

When she had time, which wasn't often, she baked her own bread. That day she baked bread, made a caraway cake, a large apple tart and mixed batter for Yorkshire pudding. The afternoon was humid, airless and thundery. The voices of blackbirds from the beech-wood sounded warm and choked. The kitchen had the same humid choked air too and she was glad to sit with the door open, on the threshold, to scrape the potatoes and shell the beans.

Just before six o'clock a total stranger walked up the path from the wood: a young fair-haired man in a blue serge suit, carrying a brown canvas suitcase. For fully half a minute she failed to recognise the soldier. Then in the excitement of the moment of recognition she rushed irrepressibly forward and actually put her hands on his shoulders.

'Oh! I could kiss you. I thought you were someone else.'

'No.' He grinned, blue eyes scintillating. 'It's me all right.'

'But why the civvies?'

'Leave started at midday today.'

'And you didn't go home?'

'Thought it'd be nice to have one more evening up here.'

She took the peeled potatoes and shelled beans inside to the kitchen sink and washed them. Then she brought back another chair and set it outside, on the threshold. For several minutes, sitting here together, in silence, she and the young man in the blue serge suit behaved like strangers. This feeling, in her, was so overwhelming that at last she confessed it:

'I feel all sort of odd. I feel I just met you for the first time. You look different. So much different.'

'Yes? Well, you look the same.'

An embarrassing sense of shame overtook her. She felt sharply self-conscious of her dirty denim trousers, her old brown shirt and her gum-boots.

'Well, I shouldn't,' she said and had no idea why she said it. 'Hot, isn't it? I got some beer somewhere. You'd like that, wouldn't you?'

She went suddenly into the house, not waiting for an answer. Inside, in the little living-room, the table was laid for supper. On another, smaller table stood bottles of beer and glasses.

She ignored them and went upstairs. In her bedroom she washed her hands and face and thoroughly brushed her hair. Then, for the first time for months, she put on a green blouse, a dark brick-coloured skirt and a pair of brown leather shoes. Then she brushed her hair again, sweeping it up at the back and pinning it. Finally she put on the lightest smear of lipstick.

Then when she looked at herself in the dressing-table glass she decided that the blouse, with its V-neck, was cut too low. She hastily put on a pale green chiffon scarf, then decided that that too was not right and took it off again. She hadn't worn it since the earliest days of the war and somehow, now, it seemed fussy and dated.

She went downstairs. She felt curiously free and airy. The blouse and skirt seemed to lift her up. At the same time she was flushed and as she carried two bottles of beer and two glasses outside to the threshold her hands were clammy.

'Now *you* look different.'

It was now her turn to feel shy. A desire to withdraw herself quickly away from him sent her back to the kitchen and the stove. She opened the door of the stove.

The piece of beef was sizzling away inside. Its rich aroma filled the kitchen and he called:

'Smells good. Different from army stuff.'

'You like Yorkshire pudding?'

'You mean you're cooking this for me?'

Yes, she was, she said. She felt not merely shy but nervous now. She dallied in the kitchen, filling saucepans with water, putting them on the stove.

'Can't think why you should go to all this trouble.'

Well, in a way, she started to say – She was now almost back over the threshold. He was pouring himself a glass of beer. Towards the west, half way across the valley, two clouds like smoky mushrooms were slowly being drawn to each other, fusing into a single ominous thundery mass that shut out the sun.

It felt so hot, she said. It was awfully thundery. She felt for the scarf at her throat, remembered it wasn't there and then didn't know what to do with her hands. The supper? – it was sort of to repay him for what he'd done for her.

'Oh! that. That's nothing. I liked doing it. Made me feel at home. Just like home. You can't think what it meant.'

'I ought to put the pudding in,' she said, and went suddenly back into the kitchen, nervous again.

'It looks black out there,' he called. 'Like thunder. Wouldn't you like some beer?'

'Yes. Pour me a glass, would you?'

She fidgeted to and fro from sink to stove, putting

vegetables into saucepans. Suddenly she was again overcome by a feeling that she and the young man in the blue serge suit were total strangers.

'I've got broad beans. Do you like parsley sauce with them? or just a bit of butter?'

'Parsley sauce. Yorkshire pudding. God, now I know I'm on leave.'

'Don't count on it too much. I don't cook very much nowadays. I nearly forgot how to.'

She put the saucepans on the stove and the beef and

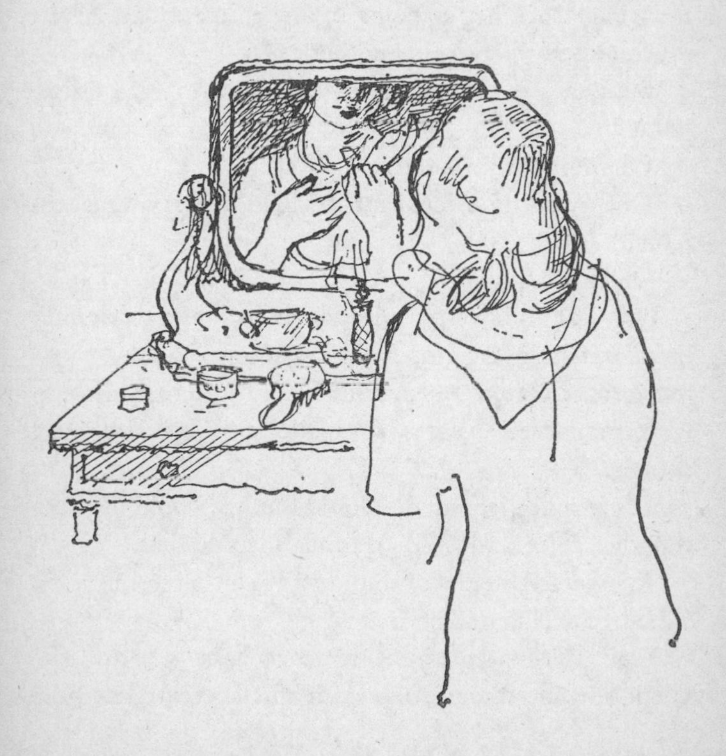

its batter back inside the stove. Again she made the gesture of fingering the scarf that wasn't there. Then she went outside again. Across the valley the clouds had moved prodigiously fast. They were now completely fused, above vivid emerald fields, into a single canopy of iron.

'I poured your beer.'

'Thanks.' She took her glass and drank. He looked at her quickly, then away at the gathering thunder clouds. In the rapidly darkening sky his eyes had a brilliant lightness that struck her as being in a way unearthly. Again she felt totally estranged and said:

'Supper won't be long now. How are you getting home?'

'Catching the milk train.'

'Oh? What time does that go? Shall I hurry things up a bit?'

'Oh! no. Midnight.'

They sat for twenty minutes or so longer, drinking beer, watching the impending ominous clouds speeding across a pattern of emerald fields set here and there with motionless figures of cattle cut brilliantly in copper.

'It's so quiet,' she said. 'You'd think it would begin to thunder. It feels odd. You'd think it would rain.'

'Are you frightened of thunder?'

'Oh! no. No, no.'

Again she made an excuse to go back into the kitchen. She had managed to skim a little cream from the day's milk and now she took a fork and nervously tried to whip it in a basin. He evidently heard the sound and came to the door and said:

'Anything I can do to help you?'

'No, no. We're nearly ready now. Well, you could whip this cream – I'm never much of a hand at it.'

She was glad to be rid of the cream. Her hands, she discovered, were shaking.

'I'd better bring the beer in,' she said. 'In case it rains.'

As she brought back bottles and glasses from outside she actually managed a confused sort of conjuring trick, drinking as she walked. A great oppressive humidity filled the air. With the heat of the stove, under the corrugated roof of the house, the little kitchen itself smouldered like an oven.

Five minutes or so later the two of them sat down at the table in the sitting-room. At this point he seemed shy again and with some slight agitation she urged him to eat while it was hot and then laughed briefly and said:

'Not that it's likely to get cold all that quick. Why don't you take your jacket off, anyway?'

'That's an idea,' he said, and took his jacket off.

This was all they had to say to each other for some time longer. Once he made a gesture of half-raising his glass as if the occasion were one of some sort of celebration but the moment passed without a word.

When the next word did come at long last it was from

her. And again, as she spoke, she fingered for the absent scarf at her neck.

'You know what I feel? I feel the war isn't on any more.'

'How?' he said. 'Why?'

Well, she said, she supposed it was something about themselves: he in his civvies and she wearing a dress for the first time for the Lord knew how long.

'Makes you feel sort of outside it. You left it behind somewhere.'

He merely nodded, earnestly eating beef.

'I suppose you could do that? Leave it behind somehow. Pretend it had never happened.'

'Wish to God you could.'

The first course of meat and vegetables being at last cleared away, he went on to eat large slabs of apple tart, with cream. Several times she poured more beer. Several times also she congratulated him on the cream. He'd done a super job on the cream.

'Listen,' he suddenly said. 'Hark at that.'

She thought immediately of nightingales and then knew that she was wrong.

'Rain,' he said. 'Listen. That's rain.'

Great solitary drops of rain, like slow loud bird-droppings, were starting to fall on the corrugated roof above.

'Strange,' she said. 'Rain before the thunder.'

Steadily the rain increased. Soon it was falling densely, a drum tattoo. Then an astonishingly distant, puny grunt of thunder came from beyond the woods, to be at once repressed like a pardonable belch and never repeated.

'They do that sometimes, these storms,' she said. 'They go away along the hills.'

'God, that's belting down.'

'That's how it does. The thunder gets away somehow but the rain gets trapped. Something to do with the hills. Might rain all night now.'

For some time they again sat without speaking, but now for the simple reason that under the drowning bombardment of rain on the roof it was simply not possible to make themselves heard. All the time the room was growing darker. She thought once of getting up to light the lamp. Then she felt that the strange, unreal, premature twilight somehow had her trapped and all she could do was to stare furtively at the figure in the blue serge suit and wait and listen.

Then he tried at last to say something. It was totally inaudible under the great clatter of rain and she almost shouted:

'Move your chair round. I can't hear.'

He didn't seem to understand this. She moved her own chair to his side of the table.

'Couldn't hear a thing over there. Shall I light the lamp?'

'Like the miser once said.' He laughed shortly. 'No need to waste money. We can see to talk in the dark.'

His laugh, for some reason, made her feel less tense. 'What were you going to say just now?'

'Oh! I – Oh! yes, something about it being a long swim to the station.'

'Oh! you've hours yet. It'll let up before then.'

'If it doesn't I'll have to be in at the deep end.'

Steadily, trapped, as she herself said, by the hills, the rain increased. At the same time, in the premature summer gloom, the little house grew more and more airless, more deeply stifled. She refrained from talking of lighting the lamp again and said instead:

'Let's sit by the door. At least we'll get some air like that.'

They took chairs and sat side by side at the open door. Already a small stream was rolling down the path of flagstones beyond the threshold. Through the gloom it was just possible to make out the woods at the edge of the farm-yard. They too had an imprisoning effect and in the great oppressive sultriness seemed to be steaming against the glowering sky.

'You'll never make it in this,' she said.

'I've got my gas cape.'

Several times, at loss for something else to say, he thanked her for the meal. Each time she would say it was nothing. She was glad to do it. It was a pleasure. Then he sat in contemplation for some time and seemed to remember something and finally said:

'What you said about the war not being here any longer. I get what you said now. I didn't at first. But I do now. I get what you mean.'

'But it's right what I say, isn't it? Suddenly you feel it's not here any more.'

'That's right.'

'You're just two people and there isn't anything else and you're sort of – I don't know – '

'Sort of in a vacuum.'

'That's it. Sort of in a vacuum. You're just two people and you're here and nothing outside matters. There isn't anybody else. There isn't any war. You're not part of anything except what's here.'

'The way you put it you're dead right.'

As he said this he turned and gave her a quick, spontaneous smile. She allowed herself to dwell on it for a few moments, disquietly. Then she felt her heart starting to pound. She actually stretched forward and put both her hands on his shoulders and said:

'I said once I could kiss you. God, and now I – '

She kissed him impetuously, with the merest brush of her lips. His response surprised her completely.

'I wanted to do that for a long time,' he said. 'But I didn't know quite – you know how I mean. About your husband – '

For some time they sat locked together in a completely silent embrace, oblivious even of the rain.

It was only when the rain, driving down more fiercely torrential than ever, actually began to splash in at their feet that she at last disengaged herself from the lock of a long embrace and said:

'Something tells me you've missed that train.'

'To hell with the train.'

'There's a bed here, anyway,' she said. 'No need to worry about that. There's always tomorrow.'

By morning the rain had stopped. The great width of sky across the valley was blue and crystalline.

When she woke just before six o'clock she lay for some time listening to strange sounds from the yard: somebody whistling, the noise of a bucket clanking on stones. During the hot clammy night she had thrown off most of the bedclothes and now lay with only a sheet over her naked body, wondering for a few brief moments what world she had woken to.

Finally she dressed, went downstairs in a daze and

stood at the threshold of the kitchen door, shading her eyes against the brilliance of morning sun. Presently she discovered that he had already done the day's milking; boiled a kettle for tea, cleared the table of its dirty supper things and was now tinkering with a spanner on the tractor.

Walking to him across the yard she found him dressed

in his army trousers, army shirt and army boots. The illusion that he was a total stranger had receded as completely as the thunder and the rain.

'Hello,' she said. 'You're about early today.'

She fully expected that he might kiss her good-morning. Nothing happened. The old shyness, she discovered, was completely back again. The blue eyes were more transparent than ever.

'I made a cup of tea,' he said. 'I think it's still hot.'

He left the spanner on the seat of the tractor and they went back to the kitchen. The tea was still hot. She poured herself a cup and then another cup for him. Arms crooked on the kitchen table, she held the cup for some minutes against her face, and then at last said simply:

'Well?'

'Well.'

'Rain's cleared the air.'

'Yes.'

She stared through the kitchen window. The entire valley shimmered with a great brilliance of early summer light. Here and there rain still sparkled on grass. The air everywhere was all intensely pure and still. And once again, she found herself in a vacuum, the war a myth, a million miles away.

'I wonder what it's going to be today,' he said. 'The weather I mean.'

'You can see a long way. Sometimes that's a bad sign.'

This was almost all they had to say before breakfast. Then half way through breakfast she said:

'You left your nice blue suit all over the place last night. I folded it and hung it up for you. You won't want to have it creased all day.'

'No.'

She got up to go to the stove for the tea-pot and in the act of pouring out tea she suddenly turned impulsively and kissed the side of his face.

In return he seemed about to say something and then was quiet again.

'I expect you're wondering about your train.'

'I hadn't thought.'

'There's a bus goes down about eleven. You could get that. It'll drop you near the station.'

'No idea what time there's a train.'

'They'll tell you at the station. I got an idea there's one about twelve.'

The morning went past, soft and quiet, all brilliant. She did some housework while he, out in the sun, tinkered with the tractor. The time for the bus, never mentioned again, went past too and with it, unmentioned also, the time of the train.

By afternoon he had fallen into a routine of jobs about the place that made it seem as if he had always lived there. He put the tractor into final order, mended a fence and did the afternoon milking. Most of the time she stood poised between an anxiety that he would miss a train and a dread that he would catch one.

About five o'clock a thin white wreath of smoke wound its way westward across the valley. She actually drew his attention to it and said:

'That's the five-ten. I do know what time that one goes. I'm not certain how they are after that.'

He had no comment to make about the train; and it was almost supper-time before she said:

'Were you thinking of getting that milk train again? It's just that – I mean I was thinking about supper. Will you stay for supper?'

Yes, he said, he would like to stay for supper.

'There's not much, I'm afraid,' she said. 'It'll most likely have to be eggs again.'

As supper-time approached she was aware of a great increasing tension in the air. There was no sign of rain or storm but the strings of her nerves started to grow taut

as she began to lay the supper table and once again her hands were clammy.

'I'll just give that suit of yours another brush. It was creased all over. I could run the iron over that shirt of yours too if you liked.'

Not to worry, he said, not to worry.

'It wouldn't take a minute. The stove's hot – I – it really – '

Tensely, without really looking, she turned to go upstairs. As if by accident she ran into him in the centre of the kitchen. In a moment they were clenched in embrace.

'Do you want to go?' she said. 'I mean the train – '

No, he said, he didn't want to go.

In an inexpressible agony of relief she stood half-laughing, half-crying. Then once again she kissed him.

'Are you sure you don't want to go? I mean you can stay if you want to, but if – '

'I'm sure. God, I'm sure.'

The week of his leave went past. Neither of them spoke again about a bus, a train, a moment of departure, For seven whole days he became as complete a part of the little farm as the cow, the tractor, the sheep grazing on the thin pasture below yellow fringes of rock roses beginning now to bloom on the hot exposed ridge of chalk.

It was now June. Some of the passion had gone from the first frenzied singing of nightingales but on the final evening of his leave the two of them walked to the edge of the beechwood, to listen through a darkening evening of tense clear air for some occasional suspended string of song.

All the time she dreaded any mention of the following day.

Several times she tried to push it aside either by making, aloud, such remarks as 'If the weather holds I think I could get that four-acre bit cut for hay next week,' or by telling herself, silently, that isolation and loneliness could never be quite as complete, as grey and empty again. There were always the evenings. He would come up in the evenings. She could always look forward to that.

All this time she was disposed to look at it all from her own point of view. She had forgotten his own.

'God, that bloody army. Square-bashing, spud-bashing. Fatigues. Cock-eyed schemes. Guard. Bloody sergeants. Bull. God, it's all so bloody pointless. God, who invented war?'

'Let's not talk about war. I've had a bellyful of war.'

'Sorry. Didn't mean to – but if you knew how I felt –'

She knew how he felt all right, she said. She knew also, though she didn't at this moment say it, about the ecstasy of being in a vacuum. She knew, now, of how it felt to leave war behind, obliterated, as if it had never been. She knew all about that and it was a marvellous thing.

Suddenly he astounded her by a burst of anger that

cracked the silence of the evening so sharply that she actually found herself jolted into an act of looking over her shoulder, instinctively to see if someone were there, listening.

'I'm not bloody going back again.'

She was terribly quiet. Inside of herself she was aware of an awful anguish and for fully a minute she struggled to calm it.

'You mean you're going to over-stay your leave? You'll be in trouble for that.'

No, he said, no. His voice was quite amazingly shattering for someone who out of sheer shyness had so often found it hard to express himself. No, no, not that. He didn't mean that.

'Then what do you mean?'

'What I said. I'm not going back. I'm finished. It's over the hill.'

Again she was terribly quiet. At last she said:

'I'm sure that's wrong. I'm sure you can't be right about that.'

'I tell you I'm not going back.'

'They'll get you. They always do. If you run to the ends of the earth they'll get you.'

'Then they'll get me. Then I'll be in the glasshouse. Then I'll be out of it. Then I'll run again. I'll do time. But I'm not going back.'

Far above, in the darkening beeches, a nightingale started a bust of song, faded into silence and then emerged again in a long triumphant trill.

'I'm sure you're wrong. Where would you go, for a start, anyway?'

She knew the answer quite well, even before it came.

'Here. I could stay up here.'

'That lets me in.'

'Oh! all right!' – in the first flash of anger she had ever known in him he started to stride furiously towards the house – 'all right, all right. I only meant for a day – a couple of days – '

In renewed anguish she ran after him.

'I didn't mean it like that. It's all right. You can stay. For a day or two. You can stay. I didn't mean you to think I was a coward about it. Don't think that. Please don't think that.'

He stayed the night. The night became a day and the day another night and then another day. The days and nights became a week and then another week and then a third. The third became a month and the month was July.

At first she was more nervous than frightened. She felt less guilty than tense. She tried, above all, to be practicable. He was never to go outside the house when she herself was away. He was never to answer the door to callers. Not that there were many callers. Since she baked her own bread and got milk enough from the cow neither baker nor milkman called. She drew her water from a well. She had no electricity. There were no meters to read. Once or twice a week she bicycled down to the village at the foot of the hill and bought the few essential things she needed: meat or fish, sugar and butter, rice and bacon and tea, a can of paraffin.

'But don't go out. Never go out. No matter who it is. There's inspectors snooping everywhere nowadays. You got to fill in forms for this and that, everything, the way you breathe. They try to teach you farming. Oh! yes and another thing – I used to have a packman call when I first lived here. You know, on the never-never. Stockings and undies and things like that. I told him half a dozen times not to call again but he still turns up sometimes. Rides a bicycle with a sort of wicker side-car.'

She imposed on him a necessary disguise. She packed away his army uniform and boots, together with the blue serge suit, and hid the lot behind a pile of straw in the barn. In their place she insisted he wear one of her own thick green sweaters, a pair of denim trousers and gum-boots. She made him wear a scarf over his head and then, more practical still, insisted he had a bust.

'Don't forget your bust,' she would say as they dressed in the mornings and the joke became the only light-hearted thing they knew.

At first the bust consisted merely of another old sweater rolled up under the green one; but the appearance, it quickly seemed to her, was false and clumsy and instead she took a bra of her own, sewed cotton wool into the cups and insisted he wear that instead.

'Nice figure,' she said. 'Now all you got to do is let your hair grow.'

By the end of July his hair had grown well into his neck. By August it was actually curling under the edge of the scarf. It was so fair in colour that soon, from some distance away, he looked like a girl, a pure natural blonde.

'Some woman in the shop gave me a turn the other morning. Said she'd heard I had some help up here. I said it was Jill, my sister. Don't forget that if ever you're in a fix. You're Jill, my sister.'

Her insistence on being scrupulously practical forced her to get up first every morning and then, before he stirred from bed, do a tour of reconnaissance through the barn, the fields and the yard. It also sharpened her wits. She grew resourceful, then cunning.

It occurred to her, for example, that he might, for reality's sake, wear a smear of lip-stick. But this thought alone was not enough. At the shop one day she said:

'I don't suppose you've got a paler red lipstick than

mine? It's for my sister. That dark shade doesn't suit her. She's on the fair side.'

Her scrupulous insistence on detail made itself felt in other ways. With infinite care, every evening, in the kitchen, she sat and manicured his finger nails. In August, in a sudden brilliant spell of heat, when he spent entire days driving tractor and binder in a wheatfield, she made him wear dark glasses. At the shop she said:

'You had a few bath cubes when I was in here last. Sort of rose-flavoured. Any left? My sister was jealous. I used them all.'

If loneliness and isolation had formerly made her jealous too, highly defensive in possession of her little stretch of land, she was now infinitely more possessive and jealous of him. Most of the time she didn't sleep well. Most nights she lay for long periods wide and starkly awake, instinctively and remorselessly listening to any sound briefly stranger than the stir of leaves, the sound of a train, a shot or a car, the cry of an owl. Tensely she translated the merest of whispers into footsteps, the sound of a summer shower into that of clumping feet.

To these tensions were added others: mostly the fear of having a child and the constant nag of money. She still bartered eggs at the shop but now there were two mouths to feed and until she could sell her harvest corn there was a widening gap to fill. There was a six-months old bill for tractor repairs, another for fuel oil, a third for a new knife in the hay-cutter, yet another for binder twine. Sometimes long after he had gone to bed she sat up struggling with impossible arithmetic in the lamplight. Beyond the arithmetic she saw winter ahead and then beyond winter, she told herself, God knew what.

For some months she hadn't touched her marriage allowance; there was some comfort in letting it accumulate at the post office. There was always a rainy day. Now, she told herself, the rainy day had come and one September evening, shortly after supper, she was suddenly caught out unawares, talking to herself, half-aloud.

'It's no good, I'll have to – '

'What'd you say? Have to what?'

'Oh! it doesn't matter.' Then a sudden rise of tension forced her almost involuntarily to confess: 'I'll have to draw my allowance out. That's what. I didn't want to have to but – '

'But you can't do that!'

'Can't? Can't? I damn well have to. I've got a pile of bills as high as a church-steeple.'

'But that won't do – I couldn't have that.'

'What won't do? Can't have what?'

'It's living on another man's – God, I couldn't do that.'

All her many tensions suddenly burst like a central fester into anger.

'You haven't much choice, have you? You haven't much damn choice.'

He stared at her, across the lamplight, in pained bewilderment. He had never seen her angered before. In turn she stared at him with something like contempt. She saw him, for the first time,with his lengthening soft fair hair and transparently blue shocked eyes, as a woman.

This recognition, in anger, made her doubly bitter.

'I'm keeping you, aren't I? What difference does it make?' She was almost shouting. 'The money's got to come from somewhere, hasn't it, for God's sake?'

He simply sat dumb. She hardly knew what she was saying next:

'That'll be the day when I don't, won't it? Keep you, I mean. Work that one out. That'll be the day. For both of us.'

His next words came up slowly, breaking on his lips like the most fragile of bubbles.

'You wouldn't let me down now? You wouldn't give me up?'

'I could, couldn't I?' Her words were whipped out. 'I could. Don't forget it's my funeral too.'

The next moment she realised that his blue, dumb and now curiously feminine eyes were near to weeping. She started to weep too, helplessly and with great harsh sobs of reproach, her face buried into her hands.

She wanted to shout 'I can't go on with it! I can't go on with it! I can't go on any longer!'

Instead she became suddenly and terribly quiet.

'We're like two people up a tree. We're trapped. We can't get down.'

Often by early November a spell of thin searing wind began to whip in from the eastern coast, skimming down the hill like an icy water fall. While the valley below still lay green there sometimes appeared long white tongues of snow on the upper hillside. The wind sang in crackling tones through the ramparts of beeches, still not stripped of final leaves, and along the fringes of woodland the big dark yews stood out blacker than ever.

On a morning just like this she went across the snow-flaked yard to the cow-shed, milk-bucket in hand, a little

later than usual. The air was so vicious with driving wind that she told herself it was too cold to snow any more. Barton was erecting hurdles for sheltering sheep on the leeside of the yard, packing inside them a wall of straw.

Suddenly she saw two men talking together inside the gate of the yard. Both were in khaki. She almost dropped the bucket.

Seeing her, they started to walk across the yard. The taller was a lean-faced young subaltern, not more than twenty-two or three, in a trench coat, carrying a cane under his arm. The other was a sergeant, massively built but not fat, with sharp penetrative brown eyes and a well-clipped military moustache, brown too above lips that seemed continually on the verge of a smile.

'Good-morning, madam.' It was the subaltern who spoke and the very courtesy of the words might have been sinister. 'Sorry to butt in on you.'

She stared stonily. 'Good morning.'

'Wondered if you could help us.' From his trench coat pocket the subaltern produced a map. 'Doing a spot of survey.' He started to open the map. 'Not exactly what you'd call summer this morning.'

'No.'

Everything about her, from eyes to speech, finger-tips to brain, was frozen. The sergeant stood slightly aside, sizing her up, eyes penetrative, looking clean through her.

'According to our map there should be a road going down here,' the subaltern said. 'Bang through the farm. This your farm?'

'That's right.'

'Bawbey Wood Farm.'

'That's right.'

'Damn funny. We haven't mis-read, sergeant, have we?'

'No, sir. Don't think so, sir.'

The subaltern again consulted the map. The sergeant, by contrast, showed no interest in the map. His eyes instead were concentrated on exploring the contours of the woman carrying the milk-bucket.

'Damn funny. There isn't a road through here?'

'The track ends at the wood.'

'Odd. There can't be *two* Bawbey Wood Farms?'

'No.' The stiff hinges of her brain moved a fraction. 'There used to be a Bawbey Wood Grange, though. Farther along the hill. That way. It got burnt down just before the war. Struck by lightning.'

'Was it, by Jove?'

'After the fire the land was all split up and sold. We bought this bit. It was only a keeper's cottage then. Wasn't a farm. We called it the farm.'

'Ah! sergeant, much is explained.'

'Yes, sir.'

The sergeant, it seemed, was not concerned with explanations. Throughout the conversation he had been solely concerned with systematic penetrations of her figure. She was aware of being openly undressed. Once or twice he smiled.

'We?' the subaltern said. 'You mean you and your husband?'

The question, innocuous enough, chilled her more than ever.

'Yes.'

'Husband about?'

'He's a prisoner of war. With the Japs.'

The sergeant seemed positively to beam.

'Bad show,' the subaltern said. 'All alone here then?'

'No.' Out of sheer fright she spoke without thinking. She actually lifted an arm and pointed to where, on the far side of the yard, Barton was erecting hurdles. 'No. I got my sister.'

The sergeant seemed positively to beam a second time. A moment or two later the fair head of Barton, wrapped in a blue-grey scarf, suddenly appeared above the height of the hurdles and as suddenly ducked and disappeared again. The sergeant noted it with refreshed anticipation.

'Mind if I look around a bit?' The subaltern's voice was casual. 'This road foxes me a little –'

He started to walk away in the direction of the hurdles. In a vain effort to distract him she said:

'The road goes down by the old Grange all right. They used to have their own private chapel there as well. But that's gone too.'

The subaltern, without reply, disappeared in the direction of Barton. In the absence of the subaltern the sergeant seemed to preen himself a little. He sniffed at the bitter morning air as though he found it drenched with honey.

'All nice an' tucked away up here,' he said. 'Keep pigs?'

The sudden crudity of the question seemed to mock her.

'No. Why should you ask?'

'Just wondered. Plenty of swill down at the camp. Could have had some sent up to you.'

'Sorry, we don't keep pigs.'

Now her voice too was cold. The sergeant merely beamed, all coldness lost on him.

'Lot o' money in pigs. Blokes are making fortunes. Millions. Free swill. No bother. One day you got one pig. Next thing you know you got a dozen. Breed like flies. Then fifty. Then a hundred.'

'It's too cold for pigs up here. Pigs don't like cold.'

Frigidly she turned her head in the direction where Barton was erecting hurdles. There was no sign either of him or the subaltern.

'Sister older than you?'

'Two years younger.'

'Don't get much delight up here?' The sergeant seemed positively to relish the word delight. 'Not much to keep you warm, like.'

'Work does, if nothing else.'

'Dance at all?'

'Don't get time for that sort of thing.'

'Used to dance?'

'Used to.'

'Miss it? Bet there's things you miss.'

She had nothing to say.

'Sister married too?'

'No, she's not married.'

'One blonde, one brunette. I ought to bring my mate the corporal up. Make a foursome. Sister care for dancing?'

'We neither of us care much for that sort of thing.'

'Oh! come on. You're young.'

'By the time we're finished up here we're just about ready to drop into bed.'

This, it seemed to the sergeant, was a joke. He laughed with an easy, oily sense of fun.

'Well, who's against dropping into bed?'

Once again she stood frigid, aloof, not speaking. Suddenly the cackle of a hen from somewhere in the direction of the hurdles made her turn her head and she saw the subaltern coming back across the yard.

'Well, here comes Lemon Face.' The sergeant seemed to think that this too was a joke. 'That's his name. Lieut. Lemmon. Fits him all right, don't you think?'

'I don't fit names to people I don't know.'

'Oh! dear, oh! dear, what have we here?' The sergeant was gay with irony. 'What have we here, what have we said?'

Her face was like a mask against the wind.

'Oh! well, if you're going to come the old acid I can always ask your sister.'

'You leave my sister alone.'

'Well, that's for her to say. Who's to say she wouldn't mind a bit of the old Turkish? Delight, I mean.'

'Leave my sister alone. She's been ill. She's not very strong.'

'Oh! I don't like 'em strong.' The sergeant, blessed by another joke, laughed. 'I don't like 'em strong. Weak, that's how I like 'em.'

His laugh, prompted again by the easy oily sense of fun, died as the subaltern arrived.

'Well, all serene, sergeant. Road must be in the other direction. Time we cracked on.' He turned and gave a scarcely perceptible courteous bow in her direction. 'Good-bye and thank you, Mrs – is it Mrs Charlesworth?'

'That's right.'

'I thought that's what your sister said.'

The subaltern gave a half-salute and turned to go. The sergeant, breaking away from the act of undressing her for the last time, turned and followed him. A hen cackled again. There was a flurry of snow along the hill side, of flying white bullets against black yews.

She stood for what seemed an hour staring stonily at

the sergeant and the subaltern disappearing towards the ramparts of beeches. Then the bucket fell from her hands and she started running.

'You think they were after you? You think that's what they were up here for?'

Barton sat at the kitchen table, drinking tea, sometimes blowing on it. It wasn't quite a lie, she told herself, about his being ill. Sometimes, with the lengthening fair hair and the withdrawn sensitive blue eyes, he gave an appearance of being fragile.

'Did you recognise either of them? You think they recognised you?'

'Different mob. Not my mob. These are Tank Corps. We were Artillery. My mob must have moved on somewhere.'

'Then what were they doing, snooping about up here?'

'Good tank-training country up here. Just what they're looking for.'

Now and then she found herself still trembling. He, by contrast, had a surprising air of assurance and calm.

It was true, as he said, that this was good tank country. The hills repeated themselves in a series of folds, mostly rough tussocky grassland broken only by clumps of gorse and hawthorn. It was the sort of country, she sometimes said, that wouldn't keep a donkey. In winter you never saw a living soul up there.

'Did the lieutenant speak to you?' she said. 'What did he say?'

'Just wanted to know your name. I thought for a moment he was going to ask for my identity-card. That would have torn it.'

'God, we never thought of that.'

'Not to worry. Just a second-lieut. Dumb as the rest.'

'The sergeant wasn't dumb, though. It was a good job you didn't speak to the sergeant. Got eyes like gimlets. Looking right through you.'

'Sergeants are always bad types. That's the way they pick them.'

'I hope I'll never see this one again, that's for sure. Cheeky devil. Wanted to go dancing.'

'With you?'

'With you too.'

Barton, like the sergeant, was quick to perceive a joke in this. He laughed and blew on his tea.

'God, now that *would* be funny.'

'I'm glad you think so. If the officer hadn't been there he'd have had me on the floor.'

After some days numbers of tanks, like dark monstrous ants embroiled in slow conflict with each other, started to scour the hillside. The crunch and moan and whine of them blistered the dry winter air. Through areas of snow they left behind them tortuously twisted trails as of black dung droppings. Now and then a splutter of shots made puny echoes.

'I've got a feeling we're in for one of those winters,'

she said one day. Above the eastern crust of hills a skein of cloud had begun to build ominously, like dark smoke. 'I've got a feeling.'

It was December before the first snow spread downwards across the farm. Below, in the valley, the fields still lay in green tranquillity.

'I saw hare tracks,' she said one morning. 'Right slap across the yard. I'll have the gun out. That'd make a dinner or two.'

'I never touch hare.'

'Oh? How's that?'

'We never had them in our family. My mother would never have them. Something funny about them.'

'I never heard that.'

'Something superstitious. Brought bad luck or something. It was to do with some saint or other. St Peter – '

'Oh! bosh. You're getting dainty. You won't be so dainty if we get snowed up for a while. The winter before last we were cut off for six weeks up here.'

'Six weeks or sixty, I don't touch hare.'

After all he was quite right, she discovered, about the gun. It wasn't bad at close range. You could shoot a rat at close range. But when it came to a running hare or a pigeon there was, she discovered, no joy.

On a milder afternoon of melting snow she tramped about the hillside, shooting without success. Cartridges, already expensive, were now also difficult to get. There was no joy.

Going back to the farm she was startled by the sudden

sight of the sergeant of the Tank Corps coming into the yard. With him was his mate the corporal, a wiry man of ferrety appearance, with pinched shifty grey eyes.

Seeing the shot-gun the sergeant was moved to make his customary joke. It took the form of raising his hands, mockingly.

'Surrender! *Kamerad!* We give in, don't we, Stan? This is my mate, Stan.'

Stan grinned. She had nothing to say.

'Nice brace o' pheasants you got there.'

The idea of pheasants was another of the sergeant's jokes. She still had nothing to say.

'Nothing for the pot, tonight, eh? Well, not to worry. How about coming dancing instead?'

'Excuse me,' she said, and started to walk towards the house. 'I'm busy.'

She hurried to the kitchen door, snatched it open and slammed it behind her. Barton, waiting for a kettle to come to boil on the stove, was reading a paper.

'Upstairs,' she said. 'Make yourself scarce. In bed. It's that sergeant again. Quick. Anywhere.'

Barton scurried upstairs. The gun still in her hands, she stood tense in the centre of the kitchen, fearful and dazed. There was suddenly a knock on the door and the voice of the sergeant was breezy outside.

'Don't be shy, duckie. Sergeants are tame.'

The door-latch clicked and the door opened. The face of the sergeant beamed across the threshold. She greeted it with the gun half up-raised.

'Now, it's rude to point, dear. Especially with guns.'

'Don't worry. Cartridges are getting scarce. I wouldn't waste one.'

The sergeant appeared much aggrieved. He was expansive with gestures of pain.

'What,' he said to the corporal, 'do you make of that, Stan? Here we come offering Mister Frank Incense and myrrh. Dance tickets. Drinks. Eats. The Good-Time-By-All. And what do we get? The old mutton. The old cold shoulder.'

Stiffly she laid the gun on the kitchen table, without a word.

'We should have thrown our caps in first, Stan,' the sergeant said, 'shouldn't we?'

'Decent men,' she said, 'take them off.'

'Ho, ho,' the sergeant said. Again he made expansive gestures of pain. 'And all because we said "Come Dancing".'

'Thank you, we don't want to come dancing.'

'We? Speaking for your sister too? Doesn't she have nothing to say for herself? Not here today?'

'My sister's not well. She's in bed. She's had a terrible bad throat this past week or two.'

'Wants keeping warm,' the sergeant said and actually winked at the corporal, 'don't she, Stan?'

That was right, Stan said, she wanted keeping warm. That was right.

'Ah! well, some other time,' the sergeant said. They had a dance every week, anyway, down at camp. An obliquely contemptuous glance crossed his face: directed not at her, but now at the gun. Contemptuously too he picked it up, broke it, examined the barrels against the light, then put the gun on the table again.

'Come over with Julius Caesar. You want to be careful. Things like that are liable to go off at the wrong end.'

'Do you mind if I lock up now? I want to get down to the shop before black-out.'

'Take a look at that, Stan. Stan knows about guns. Take a look, Stan.'

The corporal too picked up the gun, examined it and made his own contemptuous comment.

'Christ,' he said, 'you could shoot your bleeding ear off.'

It was five minutes or more after the sergeant and the corporal had gone before she dared to go upstairs. Barton was lying on the bed in a blue dressing-gown, fair hair loose on the pillow, looking startlingly, uneasily like a girl.

'It's all right. They've gone.'

'What happened?'

'A lot of old buck and so on. Not much else. I was frightened for a bit. They wanted us to go dancing.'

'Still on the dancing? God, that makes me laugh.'

'I don't,' she said, 'see anything to laugh about.'

Downstairs she made tea, put the gun away where she always kept it under the stairs and then cut a plate of bread-and-butter. Barton sat down at the table, still in his dressing-gown. She, tired more from fright than any exertion, poured out cups of tea and then sat down at the table too, heavily.

Suddenly there was a knock on the door and then the breezy voice of the sergeant:

'Only us!'

She had no time to get up before the door opened and the sergeant and the corporal were in the kitchen again.

'We come back,' the sergeant said, 'because Stan was worried about your gun.'

She again had nothing to say. The keen eyes of the sergeant alighted with the brightest interest on Barton.

'Ah! this your sister?'

'This is my sister.'

The sergeant seemed not so much to gaze on the blonde figure in the dressing-gown as to taste it. In approval he made a small, kiss-like sound.

'Like I told you, Stan. One blonde, one brunette. Good-afternoon, miss. Nice to meet you.'

Barton simply stared. He too had nothing to say.

'Now about this gun,' the sergeant said.

'What about the gun?'

'Stan thought he might take it away. He's pally with a bloke who was a gunsmith in civvy street. He could put it right for you.'

'The gun's all right as it is. We only use it for rats.'

'You could blow your bleeding ear off,' Stan said.

'We?' the sergeant said. 'Does your sister shoot? You'll be blowing your heads off one of these days, the pair of you.'

Again the sergeant's eyes alighted with a brilliance of unrestrained curiosity on Barton.

'She tell you about the dancing?' he said to Barton. 'Like to fling 'em up one night?'

Again Barton had nothing to say.

'Reminds me of that film star, Stan. Looks good but don't have nothing to say. Garbo.'

'I tell you she's had this bad throat for the past week or two. I'll get the gun.'

The sergeant could do nothing but crow in mocking triumph.

'Stan, we won a trick! Don't tell nobody, Stan. We won a trick.'

A spell of fine, humid weather worked a miracle across the hills. Once more they became softened, tender and green. The frigid snowy air that had created such a sense of imprisonment about the little farm was replaced by a feeling of release, almost of spring.

This in turn led to a certain atmosphere of carelessness. For the last few snow-gripped days she went about on guard, fearful of a crow-shadow or the noise of a plane, constantly listening for the voice of the sergeant, a knock on the door. During all this time she made Barton stay indoors. Sometimes, for half a day, while she fed and milked the cow, fed the hens and collected eggs, he lay in bed, reading or dozing or listening to music on a small portable radio. She had no cause to resent this. The fact of his being safely out of sight increased, on the contrary, her sense of security, and at last of carelessness.

On a fine soft afternoon, some days before Christmas, she cycled down to the shop to buy her weekly groceries. Like a child with an unexpected toy, she was thrilled almost to dancing by the discovery of a tin of pilchards and a pot of gold paint. Her thoughts were on a Christmas party. Three years of Christmas at war had already blessed women, at Christmas time, with a capacity for much ingenuity. She would paint branches of yew and holly with gold. There were no limits as to what you could do with things: acorns and pine-cones, branches of rose-hips, heads of teazle seed, beech branches, skeletons of leaves. She had even met a neighbour who had wrought patterns of much beauty out of gilded fish-bones.

As she rode home, stopping on the way through the wood to break off an occasional bough of holly or acorns or yew or beech still thick with husks, her sense of carelessness became complete. She hadn't seen the tanks for days. The entire valley lay below her like a huge green pond, virgin, smoothly peaceful.

Going into the kitchen, she was met by a sight that stunned her. Barton was sitting on one side of the table in a dressing-gown, blonde hair loose; the sergeant a mere foot or so away from him. On the table stood tea-pot and tea-cups. Against a chair stood the gun.

Over the back of the chair was slung a brace of pheasants, a cock and a hen, brilliant dead necks in loose embrace.

She stood quite speechless. The absence of the corporal failed to strike her, for the moment, as significant. Half-terrified, she simply stared.

It was the sergeant, naturally, who spoke first; and equally naturally with mockery.

'Ah! spring has come. Always does in time. One way or another.'

Without a word she went into the little scullery that lay beyond the kitchen. Not really knowing what she was doing, she let her shopping basket fall into the sink. It fell with a violent clatter. The next moment her hands started trembling so violently that she was forced to make several futile attempts before she could unbutton her coat.

'Cuppa tea?' It was the sergeant's voice, breezy and crowing. 'We kept it hot for you.'

The word 'we' stabbed at her. She went upstairs. Again without quite knowing what she was doing she flung her hat and coat down on the bed. An impulse to fling herself down too was arrested by a state of cold and complete paralysis.

For fully five minutes she stood in the centre of the room in this state of cold inertia, her brain and body screwed in a vice.

At last she found herself downstairs without knowing how she had succeeded in getting there. She wandered from kitchen to scullery and then from scullery to kitchen and then back again.

'Just right to hang 'em for Christmas,' the sergeant said. 'Have to be hung.'

She hadn't the remotest idea of what he was talking about. In the scullery she stared at her basket, lying in the sink. She hadn't the remotest idea of how it had got there either.

'Gun's in marvellous nick,' the sergeant said. 'Perfect. You could pick a flea off a church-steeple.'

She was going mad, she told herself. What flea? Hang what? What flea?

She stared for a long time at the pot of gold paint that had fallen from the basket into the sink, unable to think what on earth she had got it for. Then she suddenly remembered she had left branches of yew and holly and beech, together with a few acorns and pine-cones, outside, on the threshold.

She opened the kitchen door, went outside and came back with the pine-cones and acorns. She dropped them on the table while she went into the kitchen to fetch the pot of gold paint and a new paint-brush she had bought. Then she realized that the day was rapidly growing dark. She found the oil lamp, lit it and set it on the table. The faces of the sergeant and Barton were framed close together, beyond the light.

She opened the paint pot, took the brush and started to paint the pine-cones. She still hadn't spoken a word. The tips of the pine-cones, painted, wide open after the mild dry spell of weather, looked like so many little golden ears.

It was the sergeant, again naturally, who was the first to speak.

It was very sociable, he said, wasn't it? It was very sociable like, he repeated, addressing the air.

She was still speechless. With hands that were no longer trembling now, but by contrast conspicuously stiff, she painted the little ears of more pine-cones.

Very sociable, the sergeant said again, very sociable. Here it was, pretty near Christmas time. Goodwill an' all that. You brought old Frank Incense and myrrh. You brought the old pheasants. Worth five quid if a brass farthing. And so what? Very sociable, very sociable.

Silently she went on painting the pine-cones.

'Ah! well,' the sergeant said, rather as if struggling free of some painful affliction. He supposed you had to put up with these things. No peace for the wicked. 'Eh, Cath?'

The sergeant actually made a gesture of exploration in the direction of Barton's knee.

'Good thing Cath's got blood in her veins. Eh, Cath?'

Barton gave a withdrawn, nervous smile, almost coy.

The brush travelled stiffly over the intricate surface of half another pine-cone before the sergeant spoke again.

'Decorating for Christmas Eve?'

Stiffly the brush continued its travels. The sergeant picked up an acorn, still in its cup. Deftly he shelled it from the cup. Then in his quick, oily way, before she knew what was happening, he reached out, took the brush from her hand and with a few slick light strokes gilded the acorn-cup.

'How's that, Cath, eh?' He held the gilded acorn-cup to Barton's left ear. 'Pair o' gold earrings for free. Look nice at the dance, Cath, eh?'

The sergeant picked up another acorn-cup and gilded that too.

'Pretty.' The sergeant held the two gilded acorns together between his thumb and forefinger. 'Nice pair. Pretty.'

From the gilded cups of the acorns his eyes travelled the width of Barton's woollen jumper.

'Nice pair,' he said again. 'Nice pair.'

Impotent with fury, she sat for some moments longer, sightlessly staring at the half-gilded pine-cones in her hands. Then she suddenly got up, went to the stove and started to pour herself a cup of tea.

'You coming to the dance too?' the sergeant said.

The tea was luke-warm and stale. The simple fact was enough to break her silence at last. Her words spewed out in anger.

'What dance? Whose dance? Who said anything about a dance? Who wants to dance? Leave us alone, I tell you. What do you want here?'

'The old acid again, Cath. The old acid.'

Again without quite knowing what she was doing she snatched up the gun.

'If you're not out of here in two minutes – God help me, I'll do something I'll regret, God help me I will. You said it would shoot fleas, didn't you? Bugs?'

Now it was the sergeant's turn to have nothing to say.

'That's what we've always used it for,' she said. 'Vermin.'

'Don't point that gun. Don't be bloody silly.'

Barton sat white, frightened, seemingly more fragile than ever.

'Go on,' she said, 'get out.'

'All right, you don't want to come to the dance, so don't come to the dance. But Cath's coming all right. Christmas Eve. We'll have the mistletoe out, won't we, Cath? Cath's coming.'

In fury she seized the gun by the barrels, as if about to swing it. The sergeant made six measured, uneasy strides to the door.

'And take your damn pheasants with you!' She was shouting now, her voice choking. 'Take them with you!'

She hurled the pheasants at the door. They struck it as the sergeant shut it behind him.

They fell as if simultaneously shot, as a pair, all brilliant in the lamplight.

'Take them and hang yourself with them!' she yelled. 'Go and hang yourself!'

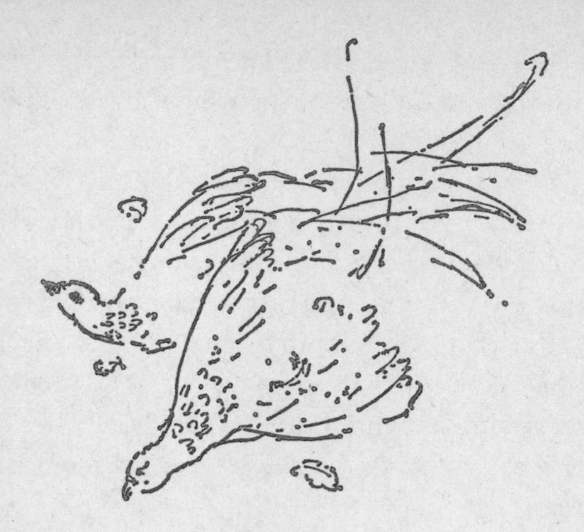

'Now what have we done?' Barton said. His voice gave an impression of being hollow, white and sepulchral. 'Where do we go from here?'

'Go? There is nowhere to go. I told you. We're up a tree. We're up a tree and we can't get down. Ever.'

For a long time she sat with her face buried in her hands, drinking from a cup of darkness inside them.

She was eventually aware that she was shrouded in more than a darkness of her own making. The light in the lamp was going down.

'Forgot to fill the lamp.' The first words she had spoken for some time were sepulchral too. 'Better do it before it gets too low –'

She wandered about from kitchen to scullery, fetching a can of oil, replenishing the lamp, wiping up with a rag the few drops she spilt about the base of the lamp.

She cleared away tea-cups, tea-pot, a few oddments that lay about the table. Once she stopped, stock-still in the centre of the kitchen, listening to what at first she thought was the sound of footsteps, then wind and rain, then what she knew was merely a gust of falling leaves.

'What in God's name made you call yourself Cath?'

'I had to call myself something, didn't I? He asked me.'

'He asked me. God.'

She sank into silence again, then beyond the barriers of complete despair into arid areas of black vacancy where she found it impossible even to think.

'Oh! I know it's my fault,' he suddenly said and made a bashing strike at the table with the flat of his hand, so that the lamp shook. 'I know. I know. Do you think I like parading about like a woman? False bloody this, false bloody that –'

'*You* don't like it.'

This was as near to any sort of coherent utterance that she got for another ten minutes or more. Several times she wanted to weep. She felt it might do her good to weep. There were times when you had to weep.

She didn't weep. There were times too when you hadn't the guts to weep. And this, she told herself, was one of them.

'I'll get you some supper,' she said at last. 'I managed to get a tin of pilchards.'

He made some muttering excuse, almost petulant, about not wanting supper, not feeling like it.

'You don't want supper.'

She passed the limits of coherence again and lapsed into yet another long silence in which she laid the table with knives and forks, bread, pepper and salt, plates and the still unopened tin of pilchards.

Then she went into the scullery and foraged about in a drawer there until she found a tin-opener. Then she came back into the kitchen and took up the tin of pilchards and he said:

'I said I didn't want supper. I don't want it, I said.'

Now she in turn made her own swinging bash at the table, bringing down the tin-opener with one hand and the tin of pilchards with the other.

'You don't want this, you don't want that. You don't like this, you don't like that. You don't like parading like a woman. God, you not only look like a woman. You're starting to *be* like one. *Think* like one. *Act* like one. You've started to get fussy and spoilt and choosy and –'

'Don't talk bloody daft.'

'I'm bloody daft, am I? Well, I wasn't bloody daft enough to make up to a sergeant, was I? Call myself Cath, promise to go to dances, put on the big flirt act? I've still got a brain or two left in my head, though God knows why.'

'It was just a gag. A joke.'

'A joke. It was a joke!'

'I always hated sergeants. I was just playing hard to get.'

'God, you'll have to play harder than hard to get with that one. He starts undressing women by remote control.'

'Why the panic, for Christ's sake? I can take care of myself.'

'You go to dances in skirts, remember? What are you going to do? Wear a chastity belt, put hand-cuffs on your bust?'

'Oh! don't bind. Don't bind.'

She picked up the tin of pilchards and the tin-opener. She made as if to begin opening the tin. Instantly he snatched it from her.

'I can do that, can't I? I can do something for myself, can't I?'

'I can do it.'

Her voice was frozen, grim and calm.

'All right,' he said, 'I won't go to the dance. We'll call it all off. Forget it. I won't go to the dance.'

'Woman's privilege, of course. Changing her mind.'

He held the tin of pilchards impotently above his head for a moment or two and then bashed it on the table.

'Only a bitch would say a thing like that. Only a bitch would say a thing like that.'

'Don't call me that. A fool if you like. A plain, big damn fool if you like. A plain big damn fool. But not that.'

Once again she reached the limits of coherence. Consumed by an enormous bitter quietness she suddenly sagged to the table. The light from the lamp seemed momentarily to blind her. Then she buried her face in her hands and once again drank, without tears, from their inner cup of darkness.

A day later, to her intense relief, snow began to fall again. She watched it from the windows of the house as a child would watch it, bewitched by transformation. Slowly at first, then in big soggy flakes and then under the driven power of a north-easter that skimmed it up into swift white vapours that piled eventually into drifts shaped against the hillside like curving scimitars, brooding white beasts or measureless glistening caverns of salt, the snow created its fast barricade of imprisonment.

When it stopped at last and she went for the first time to open the kitchen door a great avalanche fell in on her, a breaking drift the height of a man.

She was overjoyed. The sense of imprisonment created by the vastness of snow brought back a feeling of inviolate security. Again she felt herself and Barton to be cut off from the world: the world of the sergeant, the tanks, the dance, the ludicrous jest of Christmas Eve. This white imprisonment also uplifted her. Paradoxically, wonderfully, she felt free.

There were now three days to go before Christmas.

'It's going to be a white one,' she said. 'It can snow for a week. I've got everything. We won't starve. I've even got two red candles. At the shop they said they've saved a few from before the war.'

When the snow at last stopped she felt totally embalmed in its world of pure white silence. The immediate past lost itself somewhere beyond the boundaries of a great tranquillity. Without ever saying it, she regretted deeply all she had said in anger. Her tenderness for him returned.

'We said a lot of things we didn't mean,' was her way of expressing all she felt. 'We never meant all those things.'

You could, she said to him once, fairly listen to the snow silence. And had he noticed, now that the sun had come out again, how the shadows were blue?

In the white, blue-shadowed world she saw, in broad daylight, a big dog fox ambling with a sort of careless stealth across a piece of ploughed land from which strong wind had so swept the surface snow that it was now a corrugation of black and white.

'I'll have that one,' she said.

She got the gun and in gum-boots tramped out into the snow. She actually caught a second glimpse of the fox as she climbed the gate leading out of the farmyard. Then he suddenly paused, lifted his head, seemed to sniff at the air, then as suddenly doubled back on his tracks, slipped into a hedge of blackthorn and disappeared.

She started to walk across the field. A minute or so later a hare, perhaps disturbed by the presence of the fox, suddenly leapt up from the lower fringe of the hedge and began to run in great jumping bounds across the ploughed land.

She lifted the gun, fired and was sure that she hit the hare at the crest of a leap. Just to make certain she fired a second shot. Immediately the echoes of the first and second shots sprang sharp across the wide still space of snow and then, almost simultaneously, ricocheted back from the hills in a third. The hare was stone dead, blood running from its mouth, when she picked it up.

'I'll say this for the army,' she said, 'whoever fixed that gun knew what he was up to. It's never fired like that before.'

Without thinking, she flung the hare on the kitchen table. Barton had just brought in a pile of beech logs for the stove and was packing them on the hearth. Patches of snow lay on some of the logs; and across the hearth lay dirty patches of water where some snow had already melted.

Barton suddenly saw the hare and let the last of the beech logs fall with a deliberate clatter.

'Take that bloody thing out of here,' he said. 'Take that bloody thing out.'

'What's the fuss? We might be glad of it yet. The year before last we were snowed up for five weeks. I started killing the hens –'

'I told you, I don't like them things. They're bad luck. That's what my mother always said. Bad luck.'

'You should thank your good luck for a change. This snow's good luck. As long as this snow lasts nobody'll come looking for you.'

'Hares are bad luck. I don't like hares.'

'Well, you count your good luck, that's all I say. You can't ever be certain.'

'After pretty nigh six months? Don't worry. I'm buried away in some file somewhere.'

'Don't get cocky. Count your good luck, that's all I say. Don't get cocky.'

The blessing of snow lasted another day. I'm keeping my fingers crossed for Christmas, she several times told herself. All of them crossed. For Christmas Eve especially.

That night she woke in the early hours and lay listening for fully five minutes to the steady continuous sound of dripping water. She got up, went to the window, drew back the curtain slightly and knew in an instant that the wind had turned and was now blowing from the westward. Hard rain was beating on the corrugated iron roof of the house and running in spate down the gutters. She could have cried as she stood there and felt, through a slightly opened window, the moist west wind soft as milk on her face.

When daylight came rain was still falling, heavier than ever, the air mild as spring. The farmyard was a marsh of white-grey slush; the lower stretches of valley looked like a green and white archipelago of a thousand islands. The hedgerows between the fields were black again. In places even the snake-riddle of tank tracks was visible again, half in green grass, half in snow.

The desolation of thaw was repeated in a greater desolation inside herself. She hung the hare out of sight in the cow-barn, then sat for part of the morning plucking the brace of pheasants in the scullery. Obsessed by some nervous premonition she frequently tore the flesh of the birds and then sat for long intervals staring inactively at what she had done.

When Barton came in at last from cleaning out the cowbarn and said 'You might think it was spring. I'll be damned if I didn't hear a thrush singing,' she could have cried again, aware now that her premonition sprang not only from the stark fact that the disappearing snow had once again left the two of them naked but from a new fear of Christmas Eve.

'You know what I always said,' she suddenly told

him. ‘If it does come to trouble you’ll be safe in the old larder. The underground one.’

Old larder? He professed to have forgotten about the old larder.

‘You know where I mean,’ she said. ‘I took you along once. When you were first here. It’s along the hill there. A sort of cave. They used to keep the meat there in the old days, when the big house was there. It was their sort of refrigerator. It was always cold, underground. The meat would keep for weeks there, they said.’

‘Am I supposed to be classed as meat now?’

‘It’s just in case. You’ll be really safe there. Nobody knows about it. The entrancc is all grown over.’

‘How am I supposed to know when to go? Does somebody blow a bugle?’

‘I’m watching. I’m always watching.’

‘And I suppose I run like that bloody harc you shot?’

‘You’d be covered all the way by woods. It’s only about three hundred yards. Then there’s a little gate and this place is in the middle of a big clump of blackthorn. You wouldn’t be in the open for more than a minute or so.’

‘Nice place to spend Christmas.’

She wanted desperately to tell him not to talk about Christmas. The dread of Christmas Eve was again so great that half in despair she suddenly got up from where she had becn plucking the pheasants, washed her hands at the sink and said:

'It must be nearly twelve. Let's have a drink, shall we? I've got some gin. I was saving it for later but I can always get another at the pub. A couple of dozen eggs works wonders.'

They sat for an hour by the open stove in the fire-light, drinking gin with a dash of water. The gin at first filled her with a hazy calm. With the second gin she moved into positive happiness. With the third gin Barton forgot to include water. Presently her body started melting and finally she laid her head against his shoulder and said:

'That's the worst of gin.'

'What's the worst of gin?'

'Makes me feel amorous. Always makes me feel terribly amorous.'

She stroked his hair. Its extraordinary fineness, feminine as it looked, excited her still further. A moment or two later she was helping him to slip the sweater over her shoulders. In another moment her breasts were free.

Repeatedly she kept telling herself she wished it would snow again. But as she pushed her bicycle back up the hill from the shop on the afternoon of Christmas Eve there was neither snow nor wind in the sky. The air was dry and cool and still. The only snow lay in fine combs and bedraggled tatters under black hedgerows where the sun had failed to touch them.

In the kitchen Barton had been washing his hair. Now it hung in a fine bright mass almost to his shoulders, wonderfully fair, and he was brushing it. At the same time he was looking into a hand mirror propped up against a tea-pot, occasionally turning his head from side to side.

Seeing him, she simply stood staring, unable to think of a word to say.

'Like some tea?' he said. 'There's another cup in the pot.'

'No thanks.'

By this time it was becoming twilight. Without another word she went to get the lamp. As she lit it her eyes seemed, in the fresh glow of it, to assume proportions so over-large that they looked vacuous and numbed.

'Well, you don't have to gawp at me as if I'd done a crime or something, do you?'

'I don't like the word gawp.'

Suddenly she caught sight of one of her dresses, a pink chiffon one, hanging over the back of a chair, airing by the stove.

'What's my dress doing there?'

Before answering he actually picked up the mirror in one hand in order to get a closer look at himself as he carefully brushed his hair with the other.

'The corporal was here. They're picking us up at half-six.'

'*Us?*'

'The dance starts at eight. They've got drinks laid on for seven.'

'You must be stark, staring, raving mad.'

'It's Christmas Eve, isn't it? Do you good to get out and enjoy yourself a bit.'

'Good? Good? Enjoy!'

Impotently she picked up a beech log and then another and threw them into the fire. For an instant or two she was on the verge of picking up the dress and throwing that in too. Instead she turned on him with a quietness almost savage.

'Did you get this dress out for me?'

'Oh! no. It fits me a treat. I tried your green one but it doesn't go.'

'Oh! God,' she said and again, dropping into a chair, covered her face with her hands and drank from the darkness inside them. 'You poor, blind, idiotic fool.'

'Would you know I wasn't a woman?'

'*What?*'

Lifting her face from her hands, slowly and stiffly, she had the impression of struggling out of a frozen nightmare.

'Honest, would you?'

'Would I *what?*'

'With the dress on and all that, would you know I wasn't a woman?'

'I don't know anything. I don't know anything. Not any more.'

'The corporal'll be disappointed. He was on about you.'

'Was he indeed?'

'Ah! be a sport. It'll be good fun.'

So it would be good fun, would it? She must be a good sport. Not even framing the words, she sat staring mutely at her hands.

Presently Barton got up and went to the dress and turned it round, so that the other side could air at the fire. As he did so one of a pair of stockings fell to the floor and she caught a glimpse of a girdle lying on the seat of the chair. Mutely she stared at these too.

For another hour she sat at the table staring speechlessly. Then she became vaguely aware that Barton, the dress, the stockings and the girdle were no longer in the room.

She at last got up and wandered about from kitchen to scullery, scullery to kitchen and then back again. Along the edges of the mantelpiece she had already tacked a few sprigs of holly, bright with berry, a branch or two of yew and here and there a sprig of gilded acorns. Her plan had been to spend the evening finally gilding a branch of beech, decorating it with pine-cones, red candles and a present or two. It was simpler, more original than a Christmas tree. She had read about it in a magazine somewhere.

When all that was done she planned to finish preparing the pheasants, make mince pies and at last sit down before the fire with a glass of port and carols on the radio.

She did in fact, at long last, sit down before the fire; but she had forgotten about the port and there were no carols on the radio.

She was finally startled by a knock at the door. She got up to answer it, heart pounding, to find the sergeant standing outside, alone.

'Merry Christmas,' the sergeant said. 'Merry Christmas.'

Not speaking, she held open the door a little wider. Grinning, the sergeant came into the kitchen.

'Compliments of the season again and all that. Am I early? Not ready then? Don't want to be late.'

It was not her intention, she said, to be either late or early.

'Oh?' the sergeant said. 'Cath ready?'

'I don't speak for Cath.'

The voice of the sergeant was constantly breezy. There was also a certain mockery in it and also in the way he now and then rubbed his hands together.

'Not coming then?'

'I never said I was coming.'

'Corporal'll be disappointed. Got you down as his Number One Pin-up. His favourite popsie.'

'I'm not corporal's popsie.'

She fixed the sergeant with an iron stare. Greatly to her surprise he responded with a laugh. To her even greater surprise he then made a rough attempt to squeeze her shoulders.

'Ah! come on, warm up.'

Her shoulders were rigid. She had nothing to say.

'Ah! come on. Get ready. It's Christmas.'

'I would never have known,' she said, 'if you hadn't told me.'

There was no time for the sergeant to answer this before Barton came into the room. Seeing him, the sergeant seemed to give a half-suppressed gasp of surprise. She too was struck with sharp astonishment.

In the pink dress, fair hair in thick rolls at the back, shoulders half-covered with a blue shawl wrap, bust rather more prominent than usual, nails carefully manicured and touched a light shell pink, Barton looked so completely a woman that the dread in herself turned into a flash of anger and then to a stiffened sombre jealousy.

'Ah! Cath's ready if nobody else is,' the sergeant said. 'Good old Cath.'

'Not so much of the old.'

The sergeant laughed, merrily.

'Term of endearment. Term of endearment. Merry Christmas.'

'Merry Christmas.'

'Snifter before we go?' The sergeant drew a hip flask from a pocket. 'What say? Yes please? Whisky. Don't ask where I got it – no names, no pack drill.'

'I'll get some glasses,' Barton said.

He found three glasses and put them on the table. The sergeant poured whisky, generously.

'Lovely stuff,' he said. 'Had a couple in the Sergeants' Mess already. Lovely stuff. Merry Christmas. Very merry Christmas.'

Her first impulse was to refuse the whisky, then to throw it into the sergeant's face. Instead she suddenly felt a great need of it and drank it with slow relief.

The sergeant drank quickly, almost forcibly merry.

'Another? One for the road? Cath will, I know.'

Barton and the sergeant drank again. She herself stood aside, sipping slowly at her one and only drink.

'Ah! well,' the sergeant said at last. 'Better get into the old bang-bang. Borrowed a Jeep for tonight. Don't ask where. No names, no pack drill. Ready, Cath? Off then! – move to the right in pairs! –'

The whisky was talking fast. There was a glassy glint in the sergeant's eye.

'Won't change your mind, sweetheart? Corporal'll be very disappointed. Probably cut his throat. That'll be the day.'

She had only one thing to say and she addressed it coldly to Barton.

'Have you got a torch? There's no moon tonight.'

'I've got a torch,' the sergeant said. 'I'm the torch-bearer tonight. Lead on – lead, kindly light.' And then suddenly, pausing at the door: 'Haven't you got a dog, Mrs Charlesworth? You ought to have a dog up here.'

'I had one once,' she said. 'But I shot him.'

Long after the sound of the Jeep had retreated and become finally swallowed by the immense silence outside she still stood in the centre of the kitchen as if paralysed, all her dread back again.

An air-raid siren sounding far down the valley at last woke her to her senses. In a moment she turned sharply, beating her head and hands against the mantelpiece. She struck it over and over again until at last the beaten prickles of the holly leaves drew blood from her forehead and the crucified palms of her hands.

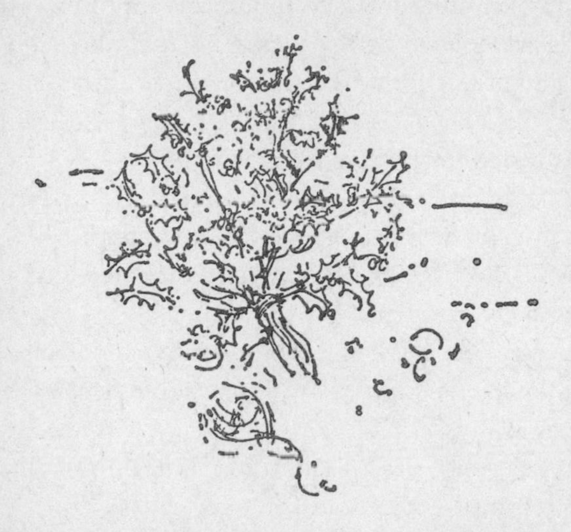

She woke early on the morning of the day after Christmas to a great surprise. Snow had fallen again in the night. As if in answer to her wish it lay all along the hillside, smooth and thin but deep enough to show, here and there, the footprints of birds. As the first daylight spread over it, thin too and still without shadow, she experienced a feeling of complete and intense relief, then of calm gladness. The illusion that snow cut her off from the world, protectively, was again complete too. Now, she told herself, with Christmas, the dance and the agonies of Christmas Eve over, all was safe again.

She went out, did the milking by the light of a hurricane lamp, collected half a dozen eggs and came back to the kitchen. The world was deadly still. A reflection of snowlight on the kitchen ceiling gave an even further illusion of seclusion and calm. The only sounds were of a kettle beginning to bubble on the stove and of Barton washing his hands at the sink in the scullery.

'It's been snowing again,' she said.

Barton had nothing to say in answer. He had in fact had scarcely a word to say in answer to anything for the whole of the previous day. The dance had put up a barrier between them.

The problem now, she told herself, was somehow to break the barrier; and snow, it seemed to her, might be the answer.

'It isn't very thick,' she said, 'but I think there's more to come.'

There was no sound from the scullery except a splashing of water.

'The wind's in the right quarter. If it stays there we'll get a packet.'

The scullery was silent.

'What would you like for breakfast?' she said. 'I'll start it now.'

'Just tea.'

'In that case I'll go up and make the bed while the kettle boils.'

She went upstairs and started to strip the bed. In the act of bouncing the pillows about and turning the sheets she suddenly paused, fascinated as she always was by snow, to look out of the window at the long calm white fringe of it extending under the beech-woods and far enough down the valley to obliterate, once again, the dirty snake-riddle of tank tracks.

Some distance below this the railway ran in a dead straight line, east to west. Half way along it was a level crossing. The gates were closed. It was the 7.58, she told herself, going towards the coast. The short, green-coached train duly came, trailing white smoke, passed the gates and went on. The gates, joined as it were by a central danger circle of red, swung back. Two cars, a tractor, a coal-lorry and a Jeep came over the line.

An odd illusion that the Jeep had in some way caught the red danger circle and dragged it across the track had her puzzled for a moment or two. Then she realised that there was not one circle but two. They were of brilliant scarlet and the Jeep was bearing them fast up the hill.

In a new rush of dread she ran downstairs, gasping:

'There's a Jeep coming up the road with two red caps in it.'

'Christ! You're sure?'

'Put your gum-boots and your sweater on. Do like I

said – go to the old larder and stop there. Stop there till I come.'

He began to drag on his boots and his sweater.

'And a scarf. This one, my woollen one. Tie it tight. It'll keep you warm.'

'Might not be nothing.'

She was actually tying the scarf for him and in the act of doing so she touched his face. It was the first physical contact between them for more than a day and it seemed to move and wake him.

'Might be, might not. If there's nothing to it I'll come for you. If there is I'll talk them off.'

She finally tied the scarf. With both hands she touched his face with the smallest gesture of affection.

'What did you do to your hands?' he suddenly said. 'I meant to ask you all day yesterday –'

'Never mind now. You go now. Quick.'

'They're all cut –'

'Never mind that.' With a gesture of desperation she again touched his face and then quickly kissed him. Her mouth was trembling. 'There's no time for talking now.'

'You won't let me down, will you?' he said, more frightened than she was, his mouth trembling too.

'Go straight along through the wood. And then turn by the clump of blackthorn. There's a double door. You used to be able to bolt it on the inside. No, I'll never let you down. I'll never do that.'

It was some time before she consciously realized that

she was alone in the kitchen, that the kettle had boiled and that she had made herself a cup of tea and was sitting at the table, drinking it. She slowly got up at last and went to the window. The yard was empty but the comforting blessed illusion of calm given by snow had vanished altogether.

Something of the calm had begun to return by the time she had drunk a third cup of tea. She was actually in the act of washing her cup at the scullery sink when there was a sharp double rap on the door.

She went to the door and opened it. Outside stood the sergeant, red cap brilliant against the snow, wearing an M.P. armband and a holster complete with revolver.

'Good morning, Mrs Charlesworth. I'd like to speak with you. May I come in?'

'Come in. There's nothing to stop you.'

The sergeant stepped over the threshold. The breezy, oily, cocky soldier of Christmas Eve existed no longer. The sergeant had become a cypher, adamant, unsmiling, correct.

'Mrs Charlesworth –'

'How did the dance go?'

Whether the subject of the dance was embarrassing or merely contemptible she never knew. The sergeant ignored it.

'Mrs Charlesworth, I'll come straight to the point. We have good reason to believe that you are sheltering a deserter here.'

'I live here with my sister. You should know. You took her to the dance.'

'We are looking for 819673 Barton A. W., Private, the Royal Artillery, absent without leave from May 14 last.'

'My sister was drunk when she came home. I've never seen her drunk like that.'

'Are you going to cooperate, Mrs Charlesworth? I should advise you to cooperate. The corporal's in the yard. I've got two men and an officer at the far end of the wood and road patrols right, left and centre.'

'You shouldn't have done that to my sister. I don't like to see women drunk.'

'Will you stop talking about your sister?' The sergeant was a flushed statue of military outrage. 'You know damn well there is no sister.'

She actually smiled.

'And how exactly did *you* find that out?'

The smile angered the sergeant still further. His voice crackled fast.

'We won't go into that. We won't go into that.'

'But you did go into it, didn't you? Or was it just some low-down, dirty, stinking trap?'

'Don't provoke me, Mrs Charlesworth. There's nothing to be gained from provocation.'

'Did you provoke Cath? or were you expecting a surprise? Provoke – I like that.'

For some seconds the sergeant remained impotently speechless. Then he collected himself with fresh severity and said:

'Don't make things more difficult, Mrs Charlesworth. We have reason to believe that you are harbouring Barton here and have been doing so for the past seven months –'

'Or perhaps you didn't want a surprise? Perhaps you're that sort of man? They tell me that kind of thing goes on in the army.'

'Keep the personal insults, Mrs Charlesworth. I am not here to be personally insulted. I am here to do a certain duty and I am going to do it.'

'Personal insult, was it? Good. Give me time and I might think up another.'

Time, she kept telling herself, was what she needed most. Contempt had given her a certain outward appearance of calm.

'Is Barton in the house, Mrs Charlesworth?'

'He is not.'

'Is that the truth?'

'That's the truth.'

'It's much better to tell the truth. Where is he?'

'Search the place. You've got plenty of men.'

The sergeant seemed to sigh.

'I must tell you, Mrs Charlesworth, that we had your place under observation all day yesterday Christmas Day. Some men missed their Christmas dinner because of it.'

'Poor things. No Christmas pudding. No mistletoe. No kissing among the soldiers.'

'Mrs Charlesworth!' The sergeant almost sprang to

attention, as if about to deliver the severest of orders. 'Do I have to remind you that it is a very serious offence to harbour a deserter?'

Time, she kept telling herself, time.

'Do I, Mrs Charlesworth?'

Before she could answer the sergeant's thundered question there was a knock on the door.

'In!' the sergeant yelled. The door opened immediately. In came the corporal, red-capped too.

'Excuse me, sergeant. Barton spotted leaving the wood about seven minutes ago.'

'Good. Which way?'

'That way.' The corporal pointed eastward. Instinctively she followed his sign of direction and the sergeant said:

'It would have saved us a lot of trouble if you'd have helped us, Mrs Charlesworth. And you too. I don't have to remind you of the penalties of harbouring a deserter?'

'Don't worry. I've been to my own funeral many times.'

'Right corporal. I'll go myself. I want this one for myself.' His quick eye alighted on the key in the lock of the kitchen door. He snatched it out, gave it to the corporal and said: 'Lock the door and stay outside. *Outside*, mind you. And see that Mrs Charlesworth doesn't leave on any account.'

There might still be time, there might still be time, she told herself; but as if knowing quite well that she had at last run out of time she stood quiet in the centre of the kitchen, expressionless, mute and at last resigned.

Still half in anger, the sergeant swung out of the kitchen. A moment later he was back again.

'Husband a prisoner with the Japs, too, my God. Oh! come all ye faithful.'

She heard the key turn in the lock. It was exactly like a black shadow turning in her mind. With pitiless calm she stood for a few moments longer in the centre of the kitchen and then seemed abruptly to make up her mind about something and went upstairs.

For some ten minutes or so she stood at the window, staring down at the snow. It had great beauty, the snow, she told herself, a great peacefulness. It was everywhere pure and crisp. Nothing but the footprints of birds had come to disfigure and disturb it.

Then she caught sight of a red cap advancing across the field beyond the farm. The red cap, she saw presently, belonged to the sergeant and with the sergeant, hand-cuffed to him, was Barton.

The recollection of the sergeant's final words went searing through her again in a great flash of anger and bitterness. She stared for a few moments longer at the two advancing men and her brown eyes had once again the lost transparency of the eyes of dead birds imprisoned in glass cases.

Then she went downstairs and got the shot-gun. She lifted the sash of the window and levelled the gun over the sill. The sun was breaking through a little now and the light on the snow was very brilliant.

She let the sergeant and Barton come to within a hundred yards of the gate between field and yard, then fifty, then to the gate. Then she let them climb the gate. She could see the handcuffs quite clearly now.

When the two men were rather less than twenty yards from the house she took a long, level aim on the sergeant. Then she fired. Within a second or so the two men staggered forward like idiot dolls. Then Barton was lying in the snow and the sergeant was half-crouching over him, shouting.

She fired again, instantly. The sergeant fell by the side of Barton, red cap dropping clear. The sound of shots hit the hillside, ricocheted back and seemed finally to create, as when she had shot the hare, a triple echo.

After that it was very quiet on the hills and the cap of the dead sergeant was very scarlet on the snow.

MORE ABOUT PENGUINS

Penguinews, which appears every month, contains details of all the new books issued by Penguins as they are published. From time to time it is supplemented by *Penguins in Print*, which is a complete list of all available books published by Penguins. (There are well over three thousand of these.)

A specimen copy of *Penguinews* will be sent to you free on request, and you can become a subscriber for the price of the postage. For a year's issues (including the complete lists) please send 30p if you live in the United Kingdom, or 60p if you live elsewhere. Just write to Dept EP, Penguin Books Ltd, Harmondsworth, Middlesex, enclosing a cheque or postal order, and your name will be added to the mailing list.

Note: *Penguinews* and *Penguins in Print* are not available in the U.S.A. or Canada

THE GO-BETWEEN

L. P. Hartley

'Of all the novels L. P. Hartley has written I think *The Go-Between* is the best . . . It is in what is to me the best tradition of fiction' – John Betjeman in the *Daily Telegraph*

In one of the first and finest of the post-war studies of early adolescence, a boy of twelve describes a summer visit to a Norfolk country house at the beginning of the century. Not yet equipped to understand the behaviour of adults, he is guiltily involved in a tragic drama between three grown-up people. The author forcefully conveys the intensity of an emotional experience which breeds a lasting mistrust of life.

H. E. BATES

THE DISTANT HORNS OF SUMMER

James's new nanny was seventeen years old and almost as innocent as he was. Life was good together. She entered into his imaginary world. She made friends with his invisible 'mates', Mr Pimm and Mr Monday. Then Mr Ainsworth came along. From the very beginning James's new nanny gave more attention to him. She even played silly games with him . . . like taking off their clothes together. It was enough to make a boy leave home . . .

A MOMENT IN TIME

'There would have to be
a war in a summer like this'

She was still in her teens when they came to fight a war in the air. Day by precarious day, she shared with these dedicated youngsters – hardly more than boys – dangers unbearably heightened by the peace of the English countryside.

THE WEDDING PARTY

A collection of thirteen short stories ranging from the humour of *The Picnic* and *Early One Morning* to the tragedy of *The Primrose Place* and the drama of sorrow and beauty of *The Wedding Party*.

H. E. BATES

FAIR STOOD THE WIND FOR FRANCE

'Perhaps the finest novel of the war ... The scenes are exquisitely done and the characters – tenderly and beautifully drawn – are an epitome of all that is best in the youth of the two countries. This is a fine, lovely book which makes the heart beat with pride' – *Daily Telegraph*

DULCIMA

Dulcima is beautiful and determined ... Dulcima wants money ... and Dulcima is in terrible danger ...

THE WILD CHERRY TREE

In each of these ten stories H. E. Bates evokes places and defines a life full of oddities and curiosities you could never before have imagined.

Also available

SEVEN BY FIVE

H. E. BATES'S
BEST-SELLING 'LARKIN' BOOKS

THE DARLING BUDS OF MAY

Introducing the Larkins, a family with a place in popular mythology.
Here they come, in the first of their hilarious rural adventures, crashing their way through the English countryside in the wake of Pa, the quick-eyed golden-hearted junk-dealer, and Ma, with a mouthful of crisps and a laugh like a jelly.

A BREATH OF FRENCH AIR

They're here again – the indestructible Larkins; this time, with Baby Oscar, the Rolls, and Ma's unmarried passport, they're off to France. And with H. E. Bates, you may be sure, there's no French without tears of laughter.

WHEN THE GREEN WOODS LAUGH

In the third of the Larkin novels H. E. Bates makes the Dragon's Blood and the double scotches hit with no less impact than they did in *The Darling Buds of May*. For the full Larkin orchestra is back on the rural fiddle, and (with Angela Snow around) the Brigadier may be too old to ride, but he's young enough to fall. 'Pa is as sexy, genial, generous, and boozy as ever. Ma is a worthy match for him in all these qualities' – *The Times*

OH! TO BE IN ENGLAND*

Are you taking life too seriously?
What you need is a dose of *Oh! To Be in England* – another splendid thighs-breasts-and-buttercups frolic through the Merrie England of the sixties with the thirsty, happy, lusty, quite uninhibited and now rightly famous junk-dealing family of Larkins.

NOT FOR SALE IN THE U.S.A.
*NOT FOR SALE IN THE U.S.A. OR CANADA